ERASMUS MONTANUS

LUDVIG HOLBERG

translated by
Petter Naess

INTRODUCTION

A. LUDVIG HOLBERG: LIFE AND WORKS

Ludvig Holberg, a Dano-Norwegian dramatist, essayist, and historian, was born 3 December 1684 in Bergen, Norway and died 28 January 1754 in Copenhagen, Denmark.

After attending the Bergen Grammar School and the University of Copenhagen, young Holberg gave way to his wanderlust, visiting Holland in 1704–05, and England in 1706–08, where he studied at the Bodleian Library at Oxford and received lasting impressions of English Enlightenment. He traveled to France and Italy in 1714–16, a journey of great importance for his later development as a writer, and visited Paris again in 1725–26. Following his stay in England, Holberg had settled in Copenhagen, where, after 1709, he was a fellow of Borch's College, and where, in 1711, he completed his first book, a history of Europe. In 1717 he became a professor at the University of Copenhagen. His subject was metaphysics, which did not interest him and which, in 1720, he was happy to exchange for a chair in Latin Literature. Not until 1730 did he receive a professorship in his chosen field of history. From 1735–36 he was Rector of the University and from 1737 to 1751 its Bursar. A lifelong bachelor, Holberg was a lonely man whose chief enjoyment was his writing. He was also musical and played the flute and the violin. From his writings he gradually acquired a considerable income, which he invested in landed property, and as an old man he enjoyed nothing so much as caring for his country estates. In 1747 he willed these to the newly re-established Sorø Academy and as a result was made a nobleman: Holberg, who in his comedies had ridiculed all kinds of social ambition, ended his days as a Baron.

It has been said that Holberg's anger at a colleague, whom he attacked in two Latin tracts, first made him aware of his own satiric gifts. In 1719 he published the first part of *Peder Paars*, a mock heroic poem of more than 6000 lines. This parody of Virgil's *Aeneid*, in which a modern day Aeneas (Peder Paars) is driven off course and lands on the island of Anholt, gives Holberg the opportunity not only to make fun of the pagan gods, but to ridicule university disputations in Copenhagen, as well as the superstition and greed of his countrymen on Anholt. As in Cervantes' *Don Quixote*, the ridiculous in Holberg's "hero" is mixed with a certain wrongheaded idealism, and this ambivalence recurs later in his comedies. Several lines in the poem also indicate an interest in the women's cause, which is even more evident in a poem, "Zille Hansdaughter's Defense of Womankind," from 1722.

In that year a new Danish theater was opened in Copenhagen, and there on Sept. 25, Holberg's play *The Political Tinker* was performed for the first time. During the next five years Holberg composed twenty-five comedies, most of which have since belonged to the regular repertory of Danish and Norwegian theaters. Many of Holberg's plays, like those of his admired model, Molière, are dramatic portraits of a confused central character. The political tinker, with no experience in public service, wishes to become mayor of Hamburg. Jeppe of the Hill, in the comedy of that name, after drinking himself into a stupor, believes he is dead and in heaven, where he proceeds to sentence his former superiors to death. In an epilog to this play about a transformed peasant, the local baron philosophizes on the danger of giving power to the people. While on the surface these plays seem anti-democratic, their major characters have a certain dignity and facility with language that make them more than mere caricatures. In *Jean de France*, on the other hand, the ludicrous francophile of the title role lacks any redeeming qualities and, like Molière's Tartuffe, is chased away rather than reformed, while Vielgeschrey of *The Fussy Man* has again something of the idealist in him. That is also the case with Erasmus Montanus, a farmer's son recently returned from the university, who terrorizes parents, neighbors, and in-laws with his new learning. Though in himself a ridiculous character, his enforced Galileo-style recantation (he believes the Earth is round rather than flat) is not without tragic connotations, and this double vision in many of Holberg's comedies could be seen as blurring the contours of the genre. Some critics, however, have felt that Holberg, by adding "human" dimensions to his comic characters, sometimes even improves upon the characterizations of his master Molière. In addition to these "comedies of character," Holberg produced a number of plays that are better termed "comedies of intrigue," and for which the Italian *Commedia dell'arte*, rather than Molière, seems to have been the inspiration. They are plays in which didactic content is less important than an exciting plot or festive pageantry, as in *Henrik and Perniila*, or *Masquerades*, and in which the cunning and wit of the servant pair Henrick and Perniila are central features.

In 1727 the Danish theater in Copenhagen was closed and Holberg entered on the second stage of his writing career, publishing a number of important historical works about Norway and Denmark, the city of Bergen, the Christian Church (up to Luther), the Jews, and about heroes and heroines in history. As a historian Holberg was careful in his choice of sources. Always mindful of his readers' taste, he tried to emphasize the topical and presented history in a lively and readable style.

After the satires and comedies of the 1720s and the historical works of the 1730s, the third stage in Holberg's writing career—from 1740 to his death— is taken up with his moral writings, such as, his Latin science fiction about Niels Klim (The Journey of Niels Klim to the World Underground, 1741), his *Moral Thoughts* (1744), and his five volumes of *Epistles* (1748–54). In a cave near Bergen, Niels Klim falls through a hole into the interior of the Earth, where there is an ideal state, Potu (Utop[ia] backwards), the inhabitants of which are slow-thinking, but wise, trees, and once more the female sex seems to be favored. In Europe *Niels Klim* was Holberg's most popular book, being translated into several languages already during the author's lifetime. *Moral Thoughts* and *Epistles* consist of more than six hundred essays in the manner of Montaigne. They include Holberg's amusing accounts and opinions of himself and in the past have been much used as a source by biographers and critics. Holberg also provided a colorful memoir of his life and works in three autobiographical "letters," written in Latin and published, respectively, in 1728, 1739, and 1743 under the title of "Letter to a Person of Renown." In 1827 they were translated into English as *Memoirs of Lewis Holberg*.

Ludvig Holberg is the most important man of letters in eighteenth-century Denmark-Norway and is often referred to as the father of Danish and Norwegian literature. Interpretations of his character and temperament have varied with time and place: was he a faithful supporter of Absolutism and the status quo, or a secret revolutionary living under a repressive political system? Also, to what extent does Holberg the artist depend on the moralist, and in what degree does he adhere to the classical genres? In many ways a child of the European Enlightenment, Holberg probably saw tolerance and moderation as cardinal virtues. On the other hand, his radical views on educational reform—including education for women—and his preference for imagination over rules in literature (cf. "Epistle 347" and "Epistle 435") show his complex personality. In the history of drama his greatest admirer was Henrik Ibsen, who resembled the old master, not only in his satirical outlook and love of royal favors but in his defense of women and his modern treatment of traditional dramatic genres.

BIBLIOGRAPHY: HOLBERG IN ENGLISH

Holberg's Works:

Carol L. Schroeder. *A Bibliography of Danish Literature in English Translation 1950–1980.* Copenhagen: Det Danske Selskab, 1982.

Peder Paars. Trans. Bergliot Stromsoe. Lincoln: University of Nebraska Press, 1962.

Three Comedies. Trans. H. W. L. Hime. London: Longman, 1912.

Comedies by Holberg. Trans. O. Campbell and F. Schenck. New York: The American-Scandinavian Foundation, 1915.

Four Plays by Holberg. Trans. H. Alexander. Princeton: Princeton University Press, 1946.

Seven One-Act Plays by Holberg. Trans. H. Alexander. Princeton: Princeton University Press, 1950.

Three Comedies. Trans. R. Spink. London: Heinemann, 1957.

The Journey of Niels Klim to the World Underground. Ed. J. I. McNelis, Jr. Lincoln: University of Nebraska Press, 1960.

Selected Essays of Ludvig Holberg. Trans. P. M. Mitchell. Lawrence: University of Kansas Press, 1955.

Memoirs. Ed. S. E. Fraser. Leiden: Brill, 1970.

On Holberg:

Gerald S. Argetsinger. *The Dramaturgy of Ludvig Holberg's Comedies.* Ohio: Bowling Green State University Press, 1975.

F. J. Billeskov Jansen. *Ludvig Holberg.* Boston: Twayne, 1974.

O. J. Campbell. *The Comedies of Holberg.* Cambridge: Harvard University Press, 1914.

B. UNIVERSITY TRAINING IN HOLBERG'S TIME

[In the following "(3.1.5)" stands for "Act 3, Scene 1, Line 5"]

The University of Copenhagen was founded in the year 1479 and is, after Uppsala (1477), the oldest Scandinavian university. In Scandinavia, as elsewhere in Europe, university life was completely dominated by Scholasticism, a name commonly used for the theology of the Middle Ages. Philosphy was considered nothing more than a "servant maid of theology (*ancilla theologiae*)," since its main function was to prove the dogmas of the church. The special types of philosophy used for this purpose were metaphysics and logic, other branches of philosophy were moral philosophy (ethics), and natural philosophy—then the name for what we call science. Gradually medicine and law were added to the two original subjects, but theology continued for centuries to be the major field of study, and its prominence affected even the salaries of the professors. At Copenhagen a theologian received $150 per year, a philosopher only $80, with medicine and law professors being paid $140 and $100, respectively.

During the sixteenth and seventeenth centuries, Denmark produced a number of prominent scientists, like the astronomer Tycho Brahe and the anatomists Thomas Bartholin and Nicolaus Steno, and many of them were attached to the university of Copenhagen. On the other hand, Holberg's era — the eighteenth century — was seen as a period of decline, partly because the university, rather than exploring the new discoveries in the natual sciences, tended to remain a school of theology, teaching its students first and foremost the explication of the Bible, including the use of metaphysics and logic to defend its contents. Long before Holberg, several people, including the law professor Christian Reitzer, had called for reforms in this antiquated form of education. Hence Holberg's special merit was not so much his pioneering spirit but rather his poetic ability to portray the shortcomings of the system as graphically as we see it in Erasmus Montanus.

In Holberg's day, the University of Copenhagen had 17 professors and some 300 students. These students had come from various grammar or high schools in Denmark and Norway and, as freshmen, were referred to as *deposituri* (or russ'es, from deposit*rus*, 1.2.7). Because the students' background varied so much, they all had to take a university entrance exam, *examen philosophicum*, before embarking upon their study proper. Nearly all of them hoped to become preachers and so eventually graduated in theology. Those very few who, like Erasmus, had more scholarly ambitions, studied for the degree of Bachelor of Philosophy (*baccalaureus philosophiae*, 2.2.15), and, after passing the exam, could go on to take a masters degree or even a Ph.D.

Students attended lectures (all held in Latin!) and took notes assiduously. Another form of instruction—known to most students since their high school days—was the disputation. One person, normally the professor, acted as president or *praeses* (3.1.5) and suggested the topic or sentence to be defended or opposed. He also appointed one student to be the *respondens* or proponent of the theses, and another student to be the *opponens ordinarius* (3.1.1; there could also be one or more opponents in the audience, who were then called *opponentes ex auditorio*). As a student, Montanus must have taken courses in basic philosophy or *philosophia instrumentalis*, which consisted of logic, rhetoric, and metaphysics (1.2.1). The word *instrumentalis* tells us that this was an auxiliary science, intended to help young students to reason logically and eloquently. Within the field of metaphysics, Erasmus appears to be especially concerned about what he calls *transcendentalia*, or basic ideas. When operating with such basic ideas, it is important to observe certain distinctions (*distinctiones cardinales*, 3.1.10). There is a difference between the idea of a thing (*ens rationis*, 4.4.12) and the experienced thing (for instance the concept "horse," versus one particular horse), and this idea of a thing can also be referred to as *forma substantialis* (4.4.12, substantial form, versus accidental form) or *res* (the thing itself versus *modus rei* or the thing as we experience it, 3.1.6), or one can talk about the *quidditas* (4.4.14) or "it-ness" of a thing, as opposed to its *qualitas* or *quantitas*.

While it is true that Erasmus speaks good Latin—contradicting the poor reputation of students in the fraternity known as The Cloisters (1.4.9)—in the field of philosophy his ways of reasoning are simple, unoriginal, sometimes faulty, with examples lifted from elementary textbooks of logic; and, like many foreign language primers today, those textbooks were often full of ridiculous exercises. In his arguments with relatives and neighbors, Erasmus is operating with simple syllogisms (*syllogismus* 4.2.4), Aristoteles' name for a logically constructed deductive (i.e. from the general to the specific) reasoning. Syllogisms are constructed of at least three theses, in such a way that, if two (called premises) are set up, the third (the conclusion) must be accepted. Of the two premises, the first is called the major proposition (*propositio major*), the second the minor proposition (*propositio minor*), and the conclusion is often preceded by the expression *ergo*, meaning "therefore." During the disputations, respondents and opponents would reject (*nego majorem*, 5.2.17) or be called upon to prove (*probe majorem* 1.6.12) the premises.

Holberg had tried his hand at disputation both in high school and later. In his memoirs he tells how, as a twenty-year-old graduate who had read a book proving in 60 points that women were not humans, he tried to entertain the inhabitants of Kristiansand with suitable syllogisms from the book, until he noticed that people were not amused. He adds that, after that incident, he became a particular and life-long friend of women. However, Holberg was never a friend of disputations, not only because he was a poor disputor (scoring low in his *examen philosophicum*), but also because he saw that disputations, which were meant to be a means to obtain greater clarity, tended to become an end in themselves. As an educator, Holberg wanted to see the concentration on *philosophia instrumentalis* replaced by a new emphasis on *philosophia naturalis* and by other subjects that would serve young men in their future careers as civil servants—such as history, jurisprudence, and economics. And, like the Lieutenant in Erasmus Montanus, he was particulary concerned with the teaching of *philosophia moralis*, since it trained young people in the art of living in harmony with other members of society. In his introduction to an essay on Socrates (in *Stories of Heroes*, Vol. 2), Holberg elaborates on what he calls the "criteria of a true philosopher." These are his fourteen points : 1. Perfect learning. 2. Ability to control one's temper. 3. Courtesy and good manners. 4. Concern about promoting human welfare and happiness. 5. A will to search for truth, and courage to preach one's findings. 6. Seriousness without affectation. 7. Knowledge of self. 8. No desire for worldy or vain promotion, but rather satisfaction with one's place in society and lot in life. 9. Little regard for one's own person, learning, abilities, or virtues. 10. Gentleness and compassion vis-à-vis those in error. 11. Concern about one's own life and health. 12. A good citizen's love of country and respect for authority. 13. Patience during suffering and forgiveness for old injustice. 14. Constancy without stubbornness.

By these standards, Erasmus Montanus would certainly fail any exam for "true philosophers," and—to the extent that he is a typical student—so would the educational policy-makers at Copenhagen University. In those days many students and teachers lacked the ability to laugh at themselves and therefore found *Erasmus Montanus* offensive—this at least seems a reasonable explanation for the fact that the play was not produced until 1747: Close to 25 years after it was written! Later generations, on the other hand, have found *Erasmus Montanus* to be one of Holberg's most important works. With its emphasis on ethics (the Lieutenant's speech) and practical knowledge (Jacob's wisdom), it has influenced educational thinking in Denmark and Norway to the present day.

ERASMUS MONTANUS

LUDVIG HOLBERG

translated by
Petter Naess

THE CHARACTERS

MONTANUS

JEPPE BERG, his father

NILLE, his mother

LISBET, Montanus's fiancée

JERONIMUS, her father

MAGDELONE, her mother

JACOB, Montanus's brother

PER, the Deacon

JESPER, the Bailiff

A Lieutenant

A Corporal

ACT I

Scene I

(Jeppe alone, with a letter in his hand)

JEPPE It's a shame the deacon isn't in town; there's so much Latin in my son's letter that I don't understand. It always brings tears to my eyes to think that the mere son of a peasant has become so learned, the more so since we're not tenants of the university lands. I've been told, by people who know about learning, that he can hold his own in disputation with any clergyman around. Ah, if only me and my wife could have the pleasure of hearing him preach in these parts before we die, we wouldn't think twice about all those shillings we've spent on him. But I can tell that Per the Deacon isn't too pleased about my son coming here. I get the impression he's kind of afraid of Rasmus Berg. It's terrible with these learned people how they envy each other; it's as if the one can't stand that the other also has learning. The good man preaches beautiful sermons here in town, but it seems to me he isn't entirely free of that flaw himself. I can't understand why it should be that way—if someone says that my neighbor manages his crops better than I, should I take that to heart? Am I supposed to hate my neighbor because of that? No sir, not Jeppe Berg. Why, I do believe there's Per the Deacon now.

Scene 2

(Jeppe, Per the Deacon)

JEPPE Welcome home again, Per.

PER Thank you, Jeppe Berg.

JEPPE Ah, my good Per—if only you could explain some of this Latin in my son's latest letter.

PER Such talk! Do you mean to suggest that I don't understand Latin as well as your son? Let me remind you that I'm an old *academicus*, Jeppe Berg!

JEPPE I know that well enough; what I meant was whether you understood the new Latin, for surely that language changes just as the language of Sjaelland has done. Why, in my day we didn't talk the same way around here as we do now; what one now calls a "lackey" we called a "lad," what one now calls a "maitress" we used to call a "whore;" a "damsel" was then a "wench," a "musician" a "fiddler" and a "secretary" a "clerk." That's why I think that Latin, too, may have changed since the time you were in Copenhagen. Would you please explain what that means—I can read the letters all right, but don't get the meaning.

PER Your son writes that he is now studying his *logicam, rhetoricam*, and *metaphysicam*.[1]

JEPPE What does that mean—*logicam*?

PER That's for his pulpit.[2]

JEPPE I'm glad to hear it—just think if he could become a priest.

PER But first a deacon.[3]

JEPPE What is that second subject?

PER That says *rhetorica*, which is "liturgy" in Danish; but that third subject must be misspelled, or else it must be French—if it were Latin I'd know it right off. I am capable, Jeppe Berg, of reciting the *Aurora*[4] in its entirety; *ala*, that's a wing, *ancilla* a girl, *barba* a beard, *coena* a chamber pot, *cerevisia* beer, *campana* a sexton, *celia* a cellar, *lagena* a bottle, *lana* a wolf, *ancilla* a girl, *janua* a door, *cerevisia* butter.[5]

JEPPE You must have one hell of a memory, Per!

PER Yes, I'd never have thought I would remain for so many years in the humble post of deacon. I could have become something grander long ago if I'd been willing to attach myself to a young woman; but I prefer to fend for myself as best I can, rather than let it be said of me that I owe my position to an advantageous marriage.

---

[1] Logic, rhetoric, and metaphysics together formed the subject *philosophia instrumentalis*, which was a required subject for the university entrance exam.
[2] To study for one's pulpit: to study theology.
[3] Theologians, before they received a living, often had to serve as deacons.
[4] *Aurora Latinitatis,* meaning "The Dawn of Latin," was a word list used in Danish and Norwegian high schools. First edition 1638.
[5] *Aurora:* Per makes a number of mistakes. *Coena* means dinner, *lana* means wool, *campana* means a bell.

JEPPE But my good Per, here's some more Latin I don't understand. Have a look at this line.

PER [reads.] *Die Veneris Hafnia domum profecturus sum*.[1] That's rather high flown, and although I understand it perfectly it might easily confound another man. It says, in Danish: "There have come, *profecto*,[2] a great many russes to Copenhagen."

JEPPE Now what have the Russians come for this time?

PER They aren't Muscovites, Jeppe Berg! They are young students, called "russes."[3]

JEPPE Oh, now I understand. There's supposed to be quite some carousing when they get their "salt and bread"[4] and become students.

PER When do you expect him home?

JEPPE Today or tomorrow. My dear Per, wait here a moment while I run in to Nille, and she'll bring us out a beer.

PER I think I'd rather have a brandy, it's too early in the day for beer.

Scene 3

(Per alone)

PER To tell the truth, I'm not too pleased about Rasmus Berg coming home; it's not that I'm afraid of his learning, for I was already a seasoned student when he was just a schoolboy getting a spanking on his—pardon my saying it—backside. No, the fellows who graduated in my time were of a different mettle than they are these days. I graduated from Slagelse School with Per Monsen, Rasmus Jespersen, Christian Klim, Mads Hansen—whom we at school called Mads Pancake—and Poul Inversen—whom we called Poul Moonshine. All of them hard-headed fellows with beards on their chins, capable of disputation on any subject whatever. I've become only a deacon, but I'm content so long as I have my daily bread and under-

---

1 "On Friday I shall travel from Copenhagen."
2 Expletive used consistently by Montanus, meaning "indeed."
3 Taken from the last part of the word "depositurus" in the expression *depositurus cornua*, "about to lay down the horns." The word *rus(s)* is used even today of freshmen at Scandinavian universities.
4 As part of the matriculation ceremonies, students received salt on their tongue and wine on their head. Jeppe gets mixed up about wine and bread.

stand my office. I've increased the income considerably, and I'm better off than my predecessors were, so my successors will have no cause to curse me in my grave. People think there's not much to being a deacon, but it's a difficult office, especially if one's to make a decent living off it. Before my time people here in town thought one funeral hymn was as good as the next, but I've arranged things so that I can say to a peasant: "Which psalm do you want? This one costs so much and that one so much." And the same when it comes to scattering earth on the body: "Do you want fine grained sand, or just plain old dirt?" There are a number of other points, too, which my predecessor Christopher the Deacon had no notion of, but then he was uneducated. I can hardly understand how that fellow could become deacon, but deacon he was. Yes, Latin is of great help to a man in all his affairs. I wouldn't be without my knowledge of Latin, not for a hundred riksdalers; indeed it has brought me more than a hundred riksdalers in my calling, yes, that and a hundred more.

Scene 4

(Nille, Jeppe, Per)

NILLE [offering the deacon a glass of brandy.] To your health, Per.

PER Thank you Nille. I don't ordinarily drink brandy unless I have a stomach-ache; but then again, I usually have a bad stomach.

NILLE Do you know Per, that my son is coming home today or tomorrow? You'll find he's a man you can talk with, for the boy's not tongue-tied from what I've heard.

PER Yes, I suppose he speaks a bunch of cloister Latin.

NILLE Cloister Latin? But surely that's the finest Latin, just like cloister linen is the finest linen.[1]

PER Ha ha ha ha.

JEPPE What are you laughing at, Per?

---

1 The Cloister was the name of a fraternity for poor students at Copenhagen. Only Latin was spoken, but a Latin reputed to be particularly poor. Cloister linen, on the other hand, is a particularly fine kind of linen, woven in the cloisters of Westphalia.

PER Oh nothing, Jeppe Berg. Just another drop thank you. To your health, Nille. It's true as you say, cloister linen is good linen, but...

NILLE If the linen isn't made in a cloister, then why is it called cloister linen?

PER Yes, I suppose that's true, ha ha ha! But won't you give me a bite to eat with my brandy?

NILLE Here's a piece of bread and cheese already cut if you want it.

PER Thank you, mother Nille. Do you know what bread is called in Latin?

NILLE No, I sure don't.

PER [eating and talking at once.] It's called *panis, genitivus pani, dativus pani, vocativus panus, ablativus pano*[1]

JEPPE Good lord, Per, what a long-winded language. What is coarse bread called?

PER Coarse bread is *Panis corsus* and fine bread *Panis finis*.

JEPPE Why that's half Danish!

PER Certainly, there are many Latin words that were originally Danish, and I'll tell you why; there was an old rector at the school in Copenhagen by the name of *Saxo Grammatica*[2] who did much to advance Latin in this country and wrote a Latin Grammar, which is why he was given the name *Saxo Grammatica*. This same Saxo has greatly improved the Latin language with Danish words, for in his day Latin was so limited that one could hardly write a sentence that people could understand.

JEPPE But what does *grammatica* mean?

PER The same as *Donat*.[3] When it's bound in a Turkish binding it's called a *Donat*, but when it's bound in white vellum, it's called *grammatica*, which is declined the same way as *ala*.

NILLE I can't understand how people can remember all those things. Just hearing them talk about it makes my head swim.

JEPPE That's why learned people often as not aren't quite right in the head.

---

[1] Per's Latin leaves a lot to be desired. The forms should be *panis, panis, pane, panis, pane*.
[2] Saxo Grammaticus (around 1200), Danish historian writing in Latin. Because of his elegant language, Saxo received the epithet *Grammaticus*, meaning "linguist."
[3] Donat was the author of a Latin grammar.

NILLE What nonsense! Do you mean to say that our son Rasmus Berg isn't quite right in the head?

JEPPE It's just that I find it a bit strange, Mother, that he writes letters to me in Latin.

PER I think Jeppe is right; there is something ridiculous about it; it's as if I were to speak Greek to the bailiff, just to let him know that I could speak the language.

JEPPE Do you also understand Greek, Per?

PER Why, twenty years ago I could stand on one foot and recite the entire litany in Greek. I can to this day remember that the last word is Amen.

JEPPE I must say Per, it'll be fun when my son comes home and we get the two of you together.

PER If he wishes to dispute with me, he'll find I'm not a man to be taken lightly, and if he wants to engage me in a singing contest, he'll get the worst of it. I once sang against ten deacons, and every one of them had to give in: I out—sang them all in the *Credo*, all ten of them. Ten years ago I was offered the position of choirmaster in Our Lady's School, but I didn't want it. Why would I want that, to leave my parishioners who love and honor me and whom I love and honor in return? I live in a place where I get my daily bread and where I'm respected by one and all; indeed, the governor never comes here without sending for me, so that I can entertain him and sing for him. At this time last year he gave me two marks for singing *do, re, mi, fa, sol*. He swore it had given him more pleasure than the finest vocal music he'd ever heard in Copenhagen. Pour me another glass of brandy, Jeppe, and I shall sing the same for you.

JEPPE With pleasure! Pour another glass of brandy, Nille.

PER I don't sing for just anyone. But you are my good friend, Jeppe, and it's a pleasure to be of service. [he screeches, slowly at first.] *Do, re, mi, fa, sol, la, si, do*. Now back again: *do, si, la, sol, fa, mi, re, do*. Now you shall hear how high I can go. *Do, re, mi, fa, sol, la, si, do, re, mi, fa, sol, la, si, do, re*.

JEPPE Good heavens, that was mighty fine. Not even our little pigs can hit higher notes.

PER Now I'm going to sing rapidly. *Do, re, mi, re*—no, that wasn't right. *Do, re, mi, do, re, mi, do*—no, that was wrong, too. It's damned difficult, Jeppe, to sing so fast. But there comes Monsieur Jeronimus.

Scene 5

(Jeronimus, Magdelone, Lisbet, The Deacon, Jeppe, Nille)

JERONIMUS Good morning, brother-in-law. Do you have any news from your son?

JEPPE Yes, I think he'll be coming today or tomorrow.

LISBET Oh, is it possible? Now my dream has come true.

JERONIMUS And what did you dream?

LISBET I dreamt that I slept with him last night.

MAGDELONE There's something about dreams. Dreams are not to be scoffed at.

JERONIMUS That's true enough, but if you girls didn't think so much about men during the day, you wouldn't dream so much about them at night. I'm sure you dreamed just as passionately about me back when we were engaged, didn't you, Magdelone?

MAGDELONE True enough, but I can swear I haven't dreamt about you for years now.

JERONIMUS That's because our love is not as fiery as it once was.

LISBET But is it really possible, that Rasmus Berg will be coming home tomorrow?

JERONIMUS Oh daughter, you shouldn't let on that you're so in love.

LISBET But is it certain that he's coming tomorrow?

JERONIMUS Yes, yes, as you just heard, that's when he's coming.

LISBET How long is it till tomorrow, Father dear?

JERONIMUS What damned nonsense! These people in love act as if they were crazy.

LISBET Well, I'll be counting every hour.

JERONIMUS You might also ask how long an hour lasts, so people could assume you were completely insane. Keep such foolishness to yourself, and let us parents talk. Listen, my dear Jeppe, do you think it's advisable to let these two young ones marry before he has begun to earn his keep?

JEPPE That's up to you, I'm sure I can support them, but I guess it would be even better if he got a position first.

JERONIMUS I think it would definitely not be advisable to let them marry until then. [Lisbet weeps and wails.] Shame on you. It's a disgrace for a girl to be carrying on like that.

LISBET [weeping.] Will he soon get a position then?

JEPPE There's no doubt that he'll soon have a post. Why, from what I've been told, he's so learned he can read any book around. He wrote me a letter in Latin just the other day.

NILLE And quite a letter it was, as the deacon will tell you.

LISBET Was it that well-written?

PER Yes, not bad for one so young. He could amount to something, but he'll have to work at it. I, too, considered myself learned when I was his age, but...

JEPPE Of course, you educated people never praise one another.

PER Nonsense! Why should I be envious of him? Before he was even born I'd been up for a flogging at school on three occasions, and when he was in the fourth grade, I'd been eight years a deacon.

JEPPE One man may have a better brain than the next and learn in a year what others learn in ten.

PER In which case Per the Deacon is prepared to pit his brains against anyone's.

JERONIMUS Well, well, each may be clever in his own way. Let's go home now, children. Goodbye Jeppe—I was just passing by, and thought I might as well stop and talk with you on the way.

LISBET Oh, do let me know as soon as he arrives.

Scene 6

(Jeppe, Nille, Per, Jacob)

JEPPE What is it, Jacob?

JACOB Father, have you heard the news? Rasmus Berg has come home.

JEPPE Heavens, is it possible? What does he look like?

JACOB Oh, he looks mighty learned. Rasmus Nielsen, who drove him, swears that he did nothing the whole way but dispute with himself in Greek and Elamite and now and then with such zeal that he hit Rasmus Nielsen in the back of the neck three or four times with his clenched fist, shouting all the while "probe the major, probe the major."[1] 1 suppose he must have had a dispute with a major before he started out. At other times he would sit still and stare at the moon and stars with such rapt attention that he fell off the wagon three times and nearly broke his neck from sheer learning, so that Rasmus Nielsen laughed and said to himself: "Rasmus Berg may be a wise man in the heavens, but he is a fool on earth."[2]

JEPPE Well, let's go out and welcome him. My good Per, you come with us. It may be that he's forgotten his Danish and can't speak anything but Latin—if that's the case, you can be translator.

PER Not me. I've got other things to attend to.

---

[1] *Probe majorem* means "prove the major (proposition)," a statement heard in logical argumentation.
[2] Said of the great Danish astronomer Tycho Brahe, who wanted to steer his horses by the stars and ended up in a marsh.

ACT II

Scene 1

(Montanus with his stockings about his ankles)

MONTANUS I've been away from Copenhagen only a day, and already I miss it. Had I not brought my beloved books with me, I wouldn't be able to survive out here in the country. *Studia secundas res ornant, adversis solatium praebent.*[1] I feel as if something's missing, having gone three days without a disputation. I don't know if there are any learned people here in town, but if there are, I'll see that they're put to work, for I simply can't live without disputation. My poor parents I can hardly talk to; they're just simple people and know barely anything beyond their catechism, so I can't take much comfort in their company. The deacon and the schoolmaster are said to have studied, but I don't know to what extent—I'll see what they amount to, though. My parents were surprised to see me home so soon; they hadn't expected me to travel from Copenhagen by night. [he strikes a match, lights his pipe, and sticks the bowl through a hole in his hat.] This is called smoking tobacco student style: it's a useful invention, for a person who wishes to write and smoke at the same time, [sits down to read.]

Scene 2

(Montanus, Jacob)

JACOB [kisses his own hand and extends it to his brother.] Welcome home again my Latin brother.

MONTANUS I'm glad to see you, Jacob. But as for your being my brother, that was all right in the old days, but it just won't do any more.

JACOB How's that? Aren't you my brother?

---
1 "Studying is an ornament in days of happiness and a comfort in adversity."

MONTANUS That I don't deny, scoundrel; of course I am your brother by birth; but you must realize that you are a mere peasant lad, while I am a *Philosophiae Baccalaureus*[1] But listen, Jacob, how are things with my sweetheart and her father?

JACOB Just fine. They were here a while ago and asked when my brother would be home.

MONTANUS "Brother " again. It's not out of pride that I object, but it *profecto* won't do.

JACOB Then what should I call you, brother?

MONTANUS You shall call me Monsieur Montanus,[2] for that's what I'm called in Copenhagen.

JACOB If only I can remember it–Monsur Dromedarius, wasn't it?

MONTANUS Can't you hear? Monsieur Montanus, I say.

JACOB Monsur Montanus, Monsur Montanus.

MONTANUS Yes, that's right. Because Montanus in Latin means the same as Berg in Danish.

JACOB In that case, couldn't I be called Monsur Jacob Montanus?

MONTANUS When you have studied as long as I have and have passed your exams, you, too, may give yourself a Latin name; but as long as you're just a peasant lad, you'll have to content yourself with being called Jacob Berg, plain and simple. By the way, have you noticed if my sweetheart has been longing for me?

JACOB Yes, certainly. She was really impatient about your being gone so long.

MONTANUS You are not to address me in such a familiar manner, bumpkin.

JACOB I just meant to say that Monsur's sweetheart has been very impatient about your being absent so long.

MONTANUS Well, now I've arrived Jacob, and for her sake only; but I won't be here for long, for as soon as we've had the wedding, I'll be taking her with me to Copenhagen.

---

1 Bachelor of Philosophy, lowest of the academic degrees.
2 Erasmus Montanus is the latinized form of Rasmus Berg, berg meaning "mountain."

JACOB Won't the Monsur take me along?

MONTANUS What would you do there?

JACOB I'd have a look around in the world.

MONTANUS I wish you were six or seven years younger; then I could send you to Latin school, and you, too, could become a student.

JACOB No, that wouldn't do.

MONTANUS Why not?

JACOB Because then our parents would have to go begging.

MONTANUS Listen to what that knave can bring himself to say.

JACOB Yes, I'm full of ideas. Had I studied, I'd have become a damned rogue.

MONTANUS Why, I've been told that you have a good head. But what else would you do in Copenhagen?

JACOB I would like to see the Round Tower,[1] and the cloister where they make the linen.

MONTANUS Ha ha ha. They busy themselves with other things in the cloister besides making linen. But is my father-in-law really as wealthy as they say?

JACOB He sure is, Jeronimus is a rich old fellow and owns nearly a third of our town.

MONTANUS But have you heard whether he intends to provide a dowry for his daughter?

JACOB Yes, I think he'll set her up with a good one, especially if he's given a chance to hear the Monsur preach here in town.

MONTANUS That will never happen; I shall not humble myself by preaching out here in the country. Besides, I am interested only in disputation.

JACOB I thought it was a greater thing being able to preach.

MONTANUS Do you actually know what it means to dispute?

---

[1] Famous landmark in central Copenhagen, built by King Christian IV as an observatory in 1637–42.

JACOB Of course. I dispute every day here at home with the maids, but I never gain anything from it.

MONTANUS Yes, we have enough of that kind of disputation.

JACOB Then what is it the Monsur disputes about?

MONTANUS I dispute about learned and weighty matters, for example, whether the angels were created before mankind; whether the earth is round or oval; about the moon, sun, and stars, their size and distance from the earth, and such things.

JACOB No, I don't dispute about things like that, because those things have nothing to do with me; if I can only get the servants to work, they can say the earth is eight-sided for all I care.

MONTANUS *O animal brutum!*[1] But listen, Jacob, do you think anyone has let my sweetheart know that I've come home?

JACOB I don't think so.

MONTANUS In that case you'd better run over to Master Jeronimus's and inform them.

JACOB Yes, I could do that, but shouldn't I tell Lisbet first?

MONTANUS Lisbet? Who's that?

JACOB Don't you know, brother, that your fiancée is called Lisbet?

MONTANUS Scoundrel. Have you already forgotten everything I just taught you?

JACOB You can call me scoundrel all you want, but I'm still you brother.

MONTANUS If you don't hold your tongue, I'll *profecto* hit you over the head with this book.

JACOB It wouldn't be right to throw the Bible at someone.

MONTANUS This is no Bible.

JACOB I know a Bible when I see one, and that book is big enough to be a Bible. I can plainly see that it's not a Testament or a Catechism. But

---

[1] "Oh, you stupid animal!"

whatever it is or isn't, it's a bad thing to be throwing books at your own brother.

MONTANUS Shut your mouth, scoundrel!

JACOB Scoundrel I may be, but at least I earn with my own hands the money for my parents that you go off and spend.

MONTANUS Shut up or I'll mutilate you! [Throws the book at him.]

JACOB Ow, ow, ow!

Scene 3

(Jeppe, Nille, Montanus, Jacob)

JEPPE What's all this noise?

JACOB Ow, my brother Rasmus is beating me.

NILLE What's the meaning of this? Surely he doesn't beat you without a reason?

MONTANUS No, Mother, that's true. He comes here and picks a quarrel with me as though he were my equal.

NILLE You worthless wretch—don't you know enough to show some respect for such a learned man? Don't you know that he's an honor to our whole family? My dear and honorable son, you mustn't pay any attention to him; he's just an ignorant bumpkin.

MONTANUS I'm sitting here speculating about weighty matters when this *importunissimus* and *audacissimus juvenis*[1] comes and gets in my way. It's no child's play, having to deal with these *transcendentalibus*.[2] Not for two marks would I permit such behavior.

JEPPE Oh, don't be angry, my dear son; it won't happen again. I'm so afraid that my respected son may have become overexcited. Learned people can't take a lot of disturbances—I know Per the Deacon got overexcited once, and it took him three days to get over it.

---

1 "Impudent and audacious young man."
2 "Transcendental matters."

MONTANUS Per the Deacon, is he learned?

JEPPE He sure is. As far back as I can remember, we never had a deacon in this town who could sing as well as him.

MONTANUS He needn't be the least bit learned for that.

JEPPE He also preaches beautifully.

MONTANUS Nor does that make him learned.

NILLE Oh but, honorable Son, surely someone who preaches so well cannot be without learning?

MONTANUS Of course they can, Mama, all ignorant people can preach well, for, since they don't have any thoughts of their own to write down, they borrow sermons and learn by heart the writings of great men, which they often don't understand themselves; a learned man, on the other hand, would not use such methods but would rather compose from his own head. Believe me, it's a common error in this country to judge the students' level of learning on the basis of their sermons. But let rather a man dispute as I do—that's the touchstone of learning. I can dispute in good Latin on any matter whatever. If someone says that this table is a candlestick, I'm capable of defending the statement. If one were to say that meat or bread is straw, I could defend that too—I've done it many a time. Listen, papa, are you prepared to believe that he is blessed, who drinks a lot?

JEPPE I'd sooner think he was cursed, since drink will part a man from his sense and money.

MONTANUS I shall prove that he is blessed. *Quicunque bene bibit, bene dormit*—oh, that's right, you don't understand Latin, I'll have to say it in Danish. "He who drinks well, sleeps well"; that's true, isn't it?

JEPPE That's true enough, when I'm half drunk, I sleep like a horse.

MONTANUS He that sleepeth sinneth not, isn't that also true?

JEPPE Yes that's true. As long as a man's asleep, he doesn't sin.

MONTANUS Blessed is he who does not sin.

JEPPE That's true, too.

MONTANUS *Ergo*—blessed is he who drinks well. Mama, I shall turn you into a stone.

NILLE Such talk. Surely that would be an even greater wonder.

MONTANUS Listen and you shall see. A stone cannot fly.

NILLE No, that's true enough, unless one throws it.

MONTANUS You cannot fly.

NILLE That's true too.

MONTANUS *Ergo*—mama is a stone. [Nille weeps.] Why do you weep, Mama?

NILLE Oh I'm so afraid of turning into stone; my legs are already getting cold.

MONTANUS Don't worry, Mama, I shall immediately turn you into a person again. A stone cannot think nor talk.

NILLE That's true. I don't know if it can think, but it can't talk.

MONTANUS Mama can talk.

NILLE Yes, thank God, as the poor wife of a peasant I can talk.

MONTANUS Good. *Ergo*—Mama is not a stone.

NILLE Oh, that does me good; now I'm beginning to feel better. It sure must take a strong head to study. I don't see how your brain can stand it. Jacob, from now on you are to wait on your brother and do nothing besides. If your parents sense that you have done him wrong, you'll be beaten within an inch of your life.

MONTANUS Mama, I should like to break him of his habit of addressing me with easy familiarity; for surely it is improper for a peasant lad to assume such a tone toward a learned man; I prefer that he address me as Monsieur.

JEPPE You heard what he said, Jacob; from now on when you talk to your brother you call him Monsur.

MONTANUS I should like to have the deacon invited here today, so that I can see what he amounts to.

JEPPE Sure enough, we'll see that it's done.

MONTANUS In the meantime I will go and visit my sweetheart.

NILLE But I'm afraid it's going to rain—Jacob can carry your cape for you.

MONTANUS Jacob.

JACOB Yes, Monsur.

MONTANUS Come after me and carry my cape; I'm going out. [Jacob follows him with the cape.]

Scene 4

(Jeppe, Nille)

JEPPE We really have reason to be pleased with such a son, don't we, Nille?

NILLE We sure do; not a shilling has been wasted on him.

JEPPE And today we'll find out what how good the deacon is. I'm afraid he won't come if he hears that Ramsus Berg is here, but we don't have to let him know. We'll invite the bailiff too; he is sure to come, because he's fond of our beer.

NILLE Oh, but that's too risky, husband, to treat the bailiff; people like him mustn't get wind of how our affairs stand.

JEPPE Of course he can. Every man in this town knows that we are well-to-do people, but as long as we pay our taxes and land-rent, the bailiff can't touch a hair on our heads.

NILLE Oh, dear Husband, I wonder if it's too late to let Jacob study, too. Just think, if he could become a learned man like his brother, what pleasure wouldn't that give his old parents.

JEPPE No, Wife, one is enough; we have to have one at home who can give us a hand and work for us.

NILLE Oh, that kind of work is only good for living from hand to mouth; Rasmus Berg, who is educated, can in one hour do more for our household than the other can in a year.

JEPPE Well, it can't be helped, Mama; our field has to be tilled and the crops looked after; we simply cannot do without Jacob. Look, there he comes, back again.

Scene 5

(Jacob, Jeppe, Nille)

JACOB Ha ha ha. My brother may well be a learned man, but he is also a great fool.

NILLE You wicked scoundrel. Do you call your brother a fool?

JACOB I don't know what to call it, Mama, but it was pouring rain, and he let me walk after him with his cape on my arm.

JEPPE Couldn't you have been decent enough to say, "Monsur, it's raining; won't the Monsur put on his cape?"

JACOB It seemed strange to me, papa, that I should have to tell a person whose parents have spent so much money on getting him wisdom and manners that, when it rains on him like that, he'll get drenched: "It's raining Monsur, won't you put on your cape?" He shouldn't need me to tell him; the rain itself says as much.

JEPPE Did you then go carrying the cape on your arm the whole way?

JACOB I'll be damned if I did. I wrapped myself snugly in the cape, and that's why my clothes are completely dry. I understood that clear enough, even if I haven't used a lot of money on learning wisdom. I grasped it right away, without knowing a single letter of Latin.

JEPPE Your brother has been walking along in his own thoughts, as learned people often do.

JACOB Ha ha ha. The devil take such learning.

JEPPE Shut up, you good-for-nothing, or you'll get a curse on your tongue. What difference does it make if your brother is lost in his own thoughts once in a while, when in many other matters he can show the wisdom and fruit of his studies?

JACOB The fruit of his studies? I'll tell you what happened next on our outing. When we got to Jeronimus's gate, he walked straight over to where the watchdog stood, which would have mauled his leg had I not pulled him aside, 'cause watchdogs aren't given to looking people over; to them all strangers are the same, and they'll bite any leg they can get hold of, be it Latin or Greek. When we got into the yard, Rasmus Berg walked into the stable and called,"Hello, is Jeronimus home?" But the cows just turned their rumps to him, and none of them would say a word. And I'm sure that if any of them could talk, they would have said "What a damned idiot that fellow must be."

NILLE Oh, my dear husband, are you going to allow him to use such language?

JEPPE Jacob, you'll be in trouble if you keep talking like that.

JACOB Papa, you should rather thank me for straightening him out and getting him out of the stable and into the house. Just think, Papa, what would happen if a fellow like that went on a long journey by himself? I'm sure that if I hadn't been with him, he'd still be standing in the stable staring at the cows' rumps out of sheer learning.

JEPPE And now you're going to get a smack on your saucy mouth. [Jacob runs, and Jeppe chases him.]

NILLE What a confounded scoundrel. I've sent for the bailiff and the deacon, so that my son can have someone to dispute with when he comes back.

ACT III

Scene 1
(Nille, Montanus, Jeppe)

NILLE My son Montanus has been gone quite some time now. I just hope he returns before the bailiff leaves. He wants very much to talk to him and is curious to ask him about this and that, such as... but there he comes now. Welcome back, my dear son. Surely the good Jeronimus was more than a little pleased to see my honored son in good health after so long an absence?

MONTANUS I've spoken with neither Jeronimus nor his daughter, thanks to that knave I fell into disputation with.

NILLE What knave was that? Was it perhaps the schoolmaster?

MONTANUS No, it was a stranger, who'll be leaving today. I know who he is, although I've never had any contact with him in Copenhagen. It annoys me to death when people think they've learned everything there is to know and are in fact idiots. I shall tell Mama what happened. This knave has once or twice been *ordinarius opponens*[1]—therein lie his only *merita*. But how does he manage his *partes*? *Misere et hesitanter, absque methodo.*[2] When *Praes* at one point distinguished *inter rem et modum rei*,[3] he asked *Quid hoc est?*[4] Wretch, you should have learned that *antequam in arenam descendis.*[5] "*Quid hoc est? Quae bruta!*[6] A fellow who ignores distinctions *cardinales* and yet wants to dispute publicly!

NILLE Oh, my honored son shouldn't take such things to heart. I can tell by what you say that he must've been a fool.

MONTANUS An ignoramus!

NILLE That's for sure.

MONTANUS An idiot!

---
1 See Introduction, p. vi.
2 "Miserably, hesitatingly, and without method."
3 See Introduction, p. vi.
4 "What is that?"
5 "Before you descend into the arena."
6 "What nonsense!"

NILLE He must have been.

MONTANUS *Et quidem plane hospes in philosophia*.[1] The dog should have been ashamed of letting loose like that in the presence of so many respectable people.

NILLE He let one loose? Now that's the mark of a real swine.

MONTANUS No, Mama, he did what is worse: he publicly confounded *materiam cum forma*.

NILLE He ought to be lynched.

MONTANUS And such a fellow imagines that he can dispute!?

NILLE The devil he can.

MONTANUS To say nothing of the error he committed in his *Proemio* when he said, *Lectissimi et doctissimi auditores*.[2]

NILLE What a fool he must have been.

MONTANUS And then he places *lectissimus* before *doctissimus*, even though *lectissimus* is a predicate that can be given to any *deposituro*.[3]

JEPPE But didn't my son talk to Jeronimus at all?

MONTANUS No. Just as I was about to go into the house, I saw a fellow passing by the gate, and since we knew each other, I went over to greet him—whereupon we immediately fell to talking about learned matters and finally ended up in disputation, so that I had to give up my visit.

JEPPE I'm so afraid that Monsieur Jeronimus may be offended when he hears that my son has been at his place and gone again without talking to him.

MONTANUS Yes, well, that can't be helped. When a man abuses philosophy, he abuses my honor. I'm fond of Mademoiselle Lisbeth, but my *metaphysica* and *logica* have priority.

NILLE Oh, my dear son, what is it you're saying? Have you promised yourself to two other girls in Copenhagen? That could become a nasty business in the divorce court.

---

[1] "And such a complete stranger to the field of philosophy."
[2] "Most well-read and learned listeners."
[3] Freshmen

MONTANUS You don't understand, that's not what I meant. It's not girls I'm talking about, but two fields of knowledge.

NILLE Oh, that's different. But there comes the bailiff, and now don't you be angry any more.

MONTANUS I could hardly be angry with him; he's too simple-minded and ignorant a man for me to dispute with.

Scene 2

(Jeppe, Nille, Montanus, Jesper)

JESPER Serviteur, Monsieur. I congratulate you on your arrival.

MONTANUS I thank you, Mr. Bailiff.

JESPER I'm pleased that we now have such a learned man in town. It must have cost him a lot of brain-work to advance so far. I congratulate you, too, Jeppe Berg, on your son. Now happiness has come to you in your old age.

JEPPE Yes, that's true.

JESPER But listen, my dear Monsieur Rasmus, I'd like to ask you about something.

MONTANUS My name is Montanus.

JESPER [aside to Jeppe.] Montanus, is that Rasmus in Latin?

JEPPE Yes, it must be.

JESPER Listen, my dear Monsieur Montanus Berg. I've heard that learned people have such strange ideas. Is it true that in Copenhagen they think the earth is round? Around here nobody would believe that, and how could it be, since the earth appears perfectly flat?

MONTANUS That's because the earth is so large that one can't notice its roundness.

JESPER Yes, that's true, the earth is big, almost half the whole world, but listen, Monsieur—how many stars would it take to make a moon?

MONTANUS A moon! The moon to a star is like Pebling Pond to the whole of Sjælland.[1]

JESPER Ha ha ha ha. These learned people are never quite right in their heads. I do believe I've heard them say that the earth moves and the sun stands still. Surely the Monsieur doesn't believe that, too?

MONTANUS No reasonable man any longer doubts that.

JESPER Ha ha ha. If the earth were to move, we would have to fall down and break our necks from time to time.

MONTANUS Cannot a ship move with you on it, without you breaking your neck?

JESPER But you say the earth turns around. If the ship were to turn over, wouldn't the people then fall off?

MONTANUS No, I'll explain it more clearly, if you'll be patient.

JESPER I'm quite sure I don't want to hear anything about it. I'd have to be crazy to believe something like that. That the earth should turn topsy turvy without us falling head over heels into the great abyss!! Ha ha ha. But, my dear Monsieur Berg, why is it that the moon is sometimes so small and at other times so large?

MONTANUS If I told you, you wouldn't believe it.

JESPER Oh, go ahead and tell me.

MONTANUS It's because when the moon is full, one cuts pieces off it with which to make the stars.

JESPER That's interesting, I don't think I ever knew that. If one didn't cut pieces off it, it would grow much too big and become as broad as the whole of Sjælland. Nature certainly manages things wisely. But why is it that the moon doesn't warm as much as the sun, even though it's just as big?

MONTANUS That's because the moon is not a light, but rather made of the same dark matter as the earth and gathers its light and brightness from the sun.

---

1 Small lake outside Copenhagen, which lies on the island of Sjælland.

JESPER Ha ha ha ha. Let's talk about something else—this kind of disturbed prattle is enough to drive a man insane.

Scene 3

(Jeppe, Nille, Montanus, Jesper, Per the Deacon)

JEPPE Welcome, Per. One good man attracts another. There you see my son, who has just returned home.

PER Welcome home, Monsieur Rasmus Berg.

MONTANUS In Copenhagen I'm accustomed to being called Montanus; I ask that you also call me that.

PER So be it, it's all the same to me. How are things in Copenhagen? Did many graduate this year?

MONTANUS The usual.

PER Was anyone rejected this year?

MONTANUS Two or three *conditionaliter*.

PER Who is *Imprimatur*[1] this year?

MONTANUS What's that supposed to mean?

PER I mean who is *Imprimatur* for verse and books that are to be published?

MONTANUS Is that supposed to be Latin?

PER Yes, in my day it was good Latin.

MONTANUS Well, if it was good Latin then, it must still be. But that has never been Latin, not in the sense that you use it.

PER Why, certainly it is good Latin.

MONTANUS Is it supposed to be a *nomen* or a *verbum*?

PER It's a *nomen*.

---

[1] Per probably means the Public Censor, who puts his *imprimatur* ("may be printed") on books.

JESPER That's the way, Per, you tell him!

MONTANUS Then *cujus declinationis*[1] is *Imprimatur*?

PER All known words belong to one of eight classes, which are *Nomen, Pronomen, Verbum, Principium, Conjugatio, Declinatio, Interjectio*.[2]

JESPER Well, well! Just listen to Per when he feels like spreading his wings. That's right, keep at him.

MONTANUS He hasn't given a single answer to what I asked him about. What is *Imprimatur* in *genitivo*?

PER *Nominativus ala, genitivus alae, dativus alo, vocativus alo, ablativus ala*?[3]

JESPER So you see, Monsieur Montanus, we've got people around here as well, who know a thing or two.

PER Yes, I should think so. The fellows who graduated in my time were of a different mettle than these days—they were fellows who went for a shave twice a week and could scan all types of verse.

MONTANUS How very impressive. Today they can do that during their second year. Nowadays there are graduates from the school in Copenhagen who can write Hebrew and Chaldean verse.

PER Then they can't know much Latin.

MONTANUS Latin! If you were to go to school now, you wouldn't get beyond the bottom class!

JESPER Don't say that, Montanus. I know the deacon to be a highly educated man, and I've heard both the district bailiff and the tax collector say so.

MONTANUS Perhaps they understand as little Latin as he.

JESPER It seems to me he's more than able to answer for himself.

MONTANUS But he doesn't even answer what I ask him. *E qua schola dimissus est, mi Domine*?[4]

---

1 "Of what declension is, etc."
2 Per is quoting from *Donat*, a Latin grammar by the ancient grammarian Donatus.
3 *Alo* is wrong for *alae, ala*.
4 "From what school did you graduate, Sir?"

PER *Adjectivum et substantivum genere, numero et caseo conveniunt.*[1]

JESPER He's giving him more than he can handle if you ask me. That's right, Per, you and I shall drink a bucket of brandy together.

MONTANUS If you knew, Mr. Bailiff, what he was answering, you'd laugh till your sides split. I ask him from what school he graduated—he answers, at random, something completely different.

PER *Tunc tua res agitur, paries cum proximus ardet.*[2]

JESPER All right, now we're getting somewhere! Now let's hear you answer that.

MONTANUS I can't answer that; it's pure gibberish. Let's speak Danish so the others can understand; then they'll immediately understand what sort of fellow you are.

[Nille weeps.]

JESPER Why are you weeping, Grandmother?

NILLE It pains me to see my son beaten in Latin.

JESPER Oh, come now, Grandmother, that's not surprising. After all, Per is much older than him. It's no wonder. But let them now speak Danish, which we can all understand.

PER Good enough, whatever he chooses is fine with me. We shall put some questions to one another. For example, who was it that brayed so loud that he could be heard all over the world?[3]

MONTANUS I know of no one who brays louder than donkeys and village deacons.

PER Nonsense! Can you hear them all over the world? It was the ass in Noah's ark, because the whole world was in the ark.

JESPER Ha ha ha. Why I do believe that's the truth, ha ha ha. That Per the Deacon has a good head on his shoulders.

---

1 "Adjectives and nouns agree in gender, number, and case." *Caseo* ("cheese") is wrong for *casu*, and *conveniunt* should be *convenient*.
2 "It also concerns you, when your neighbor's wall is on fire." A quote from Horace (*Epistola* I, 18, line 84.)
3 The question is taken from a popular "Spiritual Quiz Book," first translated from German by a Norwegian clergyman in the early 1600s.

PER Who was it that slew a quarter of the world?

MONTANUS I won't answer such stupid questions.

PER It was Cain, who slew his brother Abel.

MONTANUS Prove that there were no more than four people in the world at that time.

PER Prove that there were more.

MONTANUS That's not necessary; because *affirmanti incumbit probatio.*[1] Do you understand that?

PER Of course. *Omnia conando docilis solertia vincit.*[2] Do you understand that?

MONTANUS I'm a fool to be standing here in disputation with a dunce. You wish to dispute, yet know neither Latin nor Danish, much less what *Logica* is. *Quid est logica?*[3]

PER *Post molestam senectutam, post molestam senectutam nos habebat humus.*[4]

MONTANUS Are you trying to make a fool of me? [Grabs him by the hair. they struggle. The deacon escapes and shouts, "Dunce, dunce." All leave except the bailiff.]

Scene 4

(Jesper, Jeronimus)

JERONIMUS At your service, Mr. Bailiff. But are you here? I came to see my future son-in-law, Rasmus Berg.

JESPER He'll be here in a moment. It's too bad you weren't here half an hour ago, then you could have heard him and the deacon disputing together.

JEONIMUS How did it go?

---

1 "The burden of proof rests on the one who affirms."
2 "By trying everything, diligent inventiveness wins out." A quote from the Roman author Manilius, used as a motto on the title page of *Donat*.
3 "What is logic?"
4 "After a troublesome old age, after a troublesome old age, the earth shall have us." A quote from the old German student song "Gaudeamus igitur" ("So Let's Enjoy Ourselves While We're Young"). The words *senectutam*, *habebat* should be *senectutem*, *habebit*.

JESPER Why that rogue Per the Deacon, he's cleverer than I had thought. I can tell he hasn't forgotten much, either of his Latin or his Hebrew.

JERONIMUS I can certainly believe that, since he probably never knew much of either.

JESPER Don't be so sure, Monsieur Jeronimus. He's got one hell of a sharp tongue. It's a real pleasure to hear him speak Latin.

JERONIMUS I would never have guessed. But how does my son-in-law look?

JESPER He looks damned learned; you probably wouldn't even recognize him. And he's also got a new name.

JERONIMUS A new name? What's he called then?

JESPER He calls himself Montanus, which is supposed to be the same as Rasmus in Latin.

JERONIMUS That's a disgrace. I've known many who have changed their names like that, and no good has ever come of it. Some years ago I knew a fellow who was christened Per, but as soon as he got ahead in life he decided that wasn't good enough, so he changed his name to Peiter. But that "Peiter" proved to be his undoing, because he broke his leg and died in great poverty. Our Lord won't stand for that sort of thing, Mr. Bailiff.

JESPER He can call himself whatever he likes for all I care, but I can't put up with his ideas about the Faith.

JERONIMUS What ideas are those?

JESPER It's so shocking it makes my hair stand on end just to think about it. I can't remember everything I heard him say, but I know he said, among other things, that the earth is round. What's a man to say to something like that, Monsieur Jeronimus? It can serve only to turn religion upside down and lead people away from the Faith. Even a heathen doesn't say worse things.

JERONIMUS He must have said it only as a joke.

JESPER I think that's going too far, to joke about things like that. But look, there he comes.

Scene 5

(Montanus, Jeronimus, Jesper)

MONTANUS Welcome, my dear father-in-law. I'm glad to see you in such good health.

JERONIMUS There's nothing good about the health of people my age.

MONTANUS Well, you certainly look well.

JERONIMUS You think so?

MONTANUS How is Lisbet?

JERONIMUS Well enough.

MONTANUS But what's wrong? It seems to me, my dear father-in-law, that you answer my questions so coldly.

JERONIMUS Well, I don't see why I shouldn't.

MONTANUS But what wrong have I done then?

JERONIMUS I've been told that you have such peculiar ideas. People could think you were mad or deranged, for how can a reasonable person be foolish enough to say that the earth is round?

MONTANUS But, *profecto*, it is round; I must speak the truth.

JERONIMUS The devil it is! Such stuff can't possibly come from anyone but the devil, who is the father of lies. I'm sure there's not a man in this town who wouldn't condemn such an idea. Just ask the bailiff, who's a reasonable man, if he doesn't agree with me.

JESPER It makes no difference to me whether it's long or round, but I have to believe my own eyes, which show me that the earth is flat as a pancake.

MONTANUS Nor does it make any difference to me what the bailiff or other people in this town think about the matter; I know for a fact that the earth is round.

JERONIMUS The devil it is! I think you must be crazy—you've got eyes in your head like everybody else, don't you?

MONTANUS But everyone knows, my dear father-in-law, that there are people living directly beneath us whose feet point towards ours.

JESPER Ha ha ha hi hi hi hi ha ha ha.

JERONIMUS Yes, you've good reason to laugh, Mr. Bailiff; he really does have a screw loose in his head. Just you try walking on the ceiling here with your head pointing down, and see what happens.

MONTANUS That's an entirely different matter, Father-in-law, because…

JERONIMUS I will certainly not be your father-in-law. My daughter is too dear for me to give her away to someone like you.

MONTANUS Your daughter is as dear to me as my own life, there's no doubt about that, but that I should give up philosophy for her sake and send my reason packing, that's more than you can demand.

JERONIMUS Aha, so I see you've got other ladies on your mind; well you can keep your Phyllis or your Sophie, because I'm certainly not going to force my daughter on you.

MONTANUS You misunderstand—philosophy is simply a science, which has opened up my eyes in this matter as well as in others.

JERONIMUS I should say rather that it has blinded your eyes as well as your reason—and would you say that that is a good thing?

MONTANUS There's no need even to prove that the earth is round, since there's not an educated person today who could have the slightest doubt about it.

JESPER Well, I'm sure Per the Deacon will disagree.

MONTANUS Per the Deacon! A fine fellow he is! I'm a fool to stand here discussing philosophy with you, but just to please Monsieur Jeronimus I shall nonetheless present you with a proof or two, the first being that travelers, when they've traveled a few thousand miles from here, have day when we have night and see a different sky with different stars.

JERONIMUS Are you crazy? You mean there's more than one earth and one heaven?

JESPER Yes, Monsieur Jeronimus, there are 12 heavens, the one on top of the other, until you get up to the Crystal Heaven.

MONTANUS Ah, *quantae tenebrae*.[1]

JERONIMUS When I was young I traveled to the market in Kiel on sixteen occasions, but as sure as I'm an honest man, not once did I see a different heaven than the one we have around here.

MONTANUS You have to travel sixteen times that distance before you notice it, Domine Jeronimus, because…

JERONIMUS Oh, stop talking such nonsense; that's not getting us anywhere. Let's hear your other proof.

MONTANUS The other proof is taken from the eclipse of the sun and the moon.

JESPER Now listen to that! The fellow's completely out of his mind.

MONTANUS And what do you suppose an eclipse to be?

JESPER Eclipses are special signs from the sun and moon to show that some great misfortune is about to happen on earth, and I can prove it from personal experience. Like the time when my wife had a miscarriage three years ago, and when my little daughter Gertrude died—both times there had been an eclipse just before.

MONTANUS That kind of talk drives me crazy.

JERONIMUS The bailiff is right; there's never an eclipse that doesn't have something to tell us. Last time there was an eclipse, it seemed like everything was as it should be, but that didn't last long, because 14 days later we received news from Copenhagen that six candidates had failed their university examinations, all of them distinguished persons and among them two minister's sons. If you don't hear about bad things happening at one place after an eclipse, you'll get news of them from some other place.

MONTANUS That's true enough, since a day doesn't pass without some misfortune occurring somewhere in the world. But as for those candidates, they've no reason to blame the eclipse, for if they'd studied a little harder they would have passed.

JERONIMUS So what is an eclipse of the moon, then?

---

1 "Ah, what benightedness."

MONTANUS It is simply the shadow of the earth that robs the moon of sunshine; and since the shadow is round, it shows that the earth, too, must be round. It's all perfectly natural, and since we can predict eclipses, it's ridiculous to say that they give warning of misfortune.

JERONIMUS Oh, Mr. Bailiff, this is more than I can stand—cursed was the day when your parents decided to let you study.

JESPER Yes, he's pretty close to being an atheist. I'll have to let Per the Deacon at him again—now, there's a man who speaks with force. He'll convince you, whether you want it in Latin or Greek, that the earth, thank God, is as flat as my hand. But there comes Madame Jeronimus with her daughter.

Scene 6

(Magdelone, Lisbet, Jeronimus, Montanus, Jesper)

MAGDELONE Ah, my dear son-in-law, it's a pleasure to see you home again in such good health.

LISBET Oh, my darling, let me embrace you.

JERONIMUS Easy, easy, my child, not so fast.

LISBET You mean I can't embrace my own sweetheart, whom I haven't seen for years?

JERONIMUS Stay away from him I tell you, or I'll swat you.

LISBET [weeping.] Well, I know one thing for sure, that we've been publicly engaged.

JERON1MUS That's true enough, but there's been some wrongdoing in that matter since then. You must know, my child, that when he became engaged to you he was a decent person and a good Christian. But now he has turned into a heretic and a fanatic and deserves his place in the Litany[1] rather than in our family.

LISBET If that's all that's wrong, Daddy, you'll see that we can come to terms.

---

[1] The Litany is the church prayer in which the congregation sings (among many other verses): "From all sedition, privy conspiracy, and rebellion; from all false doctrine, heresy, and schism; from hardness of heart, and contempt for thy Word and Commandment, Good Lord, deliver us."

JERONIMUS Get away from him I tell you.

MAGDELONE What's the meaning of this, Mr. Bailiff?

JESPER It's a serious matter, Madame. He introduces false doctrines into our town, says the world is round and other things like that, which I blush to mention.

JERONIMUS Isn't it a pity for his old parents, who've spent so much money on him?

MAGDELONE What?! Is that all? If he loves our daughter I'm sure he'll give up the idea and say that the earth is flat, for her sake.

LISBET Oh, my darling, say for my sake that it is flat.

MONTANUS I cannot comply with your wishes in this so long as I am in full possession of my reason. I, obviously, cannot give the earth another shape than that which it by nature is given. I will say and do for you all that is possible, but I cannot appease you in this; if my fellow students were to find out that I had advocated such ideas, they would consider me a fool and make me the object of their contempt. Moreover, we learned men do not betray our opinions but stand by what we have said, to the very last drop of our ink wells.

MAGDELONE Listen, Husband, I really don't think this is such a serious matter that we have to break off the engagement.

JERON1MUS And I, for the sake of a thing like that, would demand that they be divorced, had they already been married.

MAGDELONE Well, I should think I, too, would have some say in that matter since she's as much my daughter as yours.

LISBET [weeping.] Oh my darling, do tell them that it's flat.

MONTANUS I *profecto* cannot do it.

JERONIMUS Listen, Wife, you should know that I am the man of the house and that I am her father.

MAGDELONE And you should also know that I am the woman of the house and that I am her mother.

JERONIMUS And I say that a father always counts more than a mother.

MAGDELONE And I say not, because that I am her mother, about that there can be no doubt, but whether you…,well, I don't want to say any more, I'm getting too excited.

LISBET [weeping.] Oh, my sweetheart, won't you for my sake say that it is flat?

MONTANUS I cannot, my doll. *Nam contra naturam est.*[1]

JERONIMUS What do you mean by that, wife? Am I not just as much her father as you are her mother? Listen, Lisbet. Am I not your father?

LISBET I think so, since my mother says you are. But though I believe you are my father, I know that she is my mother.

JERONIMUS Now what do you think of such nonsense, Mr. Bailiff?

JESPER Well, I can't say the mamsell is wrong about that, but...

JERONIMUS That's enough! Let's be on our way. You can be sure, Rasmus Berg, that you'll never get my daughter as long as you cling to your misconceptions.

LISBET [weeping.] Oh, darling, tell them it's flat.

JERONIMUS Out! Out that door!

---

1 "For it is against nature."

ACT IV

Scene 1

(Montanus)

MONTANUS Here I've been suffering for a full hour the company of my parents, who with sighs and weeping would move me to give up my opinions—but they don't know Erasmum Montanum! Not if I could become emperor would I go back on what I once have said. I love Mademoiselle Elisabeth, it's true, but that I, for her sake, should give up philosophy and disavow what I have publicly maintained, that shall never happen. I hope though that things will work out all right and that I may win my sweetheart without relinquishing my reputation—because when I get an opportunity to speak with Jeronimus, so clearly shall I expose to him his delusions that he will have to give in. But there I see the deacon and the bailiff coming from my parents-in-law.

Scene 2

(Jesper, Per, Montanus)

JESPER My dear Monsieur Montanus, we've had a busy day today on your account.

MONTANUS How so?

JESPER We've been running between your parents and parents-in-law trying to negotiate a peace.

MONTANUS And so what have you achieved? Is my father-in-law to be swayed?

JESPER The last words he said to us were these: "There has never been any heresy in our family. Just say hello to Rasmus Berg"—and I'm giving you his exact words, because he didn't even say Montanus Berg—"just say hello to Rasmus Berg," he said, "and tell him that my wife and I are both decent and god-fearing people who would sooner wring our daughter's neck than give her to someone who says that the world is round and brings false doctrine into the town."

PER And really, we've always been true believers around here, so Monsieur Jeronimus is not unreasonable in wishing to break off the engagement.

MONTANUS You fine fellows! Return my greetings to Monsieur Jeronimus and tell him he commits a sin in trying to make me go back on what I have said, which is contrary to *leges scholasticas* and *consuetudines laudabiles*.[1]

PER Oh, *Dominus*![2] Would you forsake your lovely sweetheart for so trivial a thing? People will speak ill of it.

MONTANUS The common man, *vulgus*, will speak ill of it; but my *commilitones*, my comrades, will praise me to the heavens for my constancy.

PER Do you then consider it a sin to say that the earth is flat or oblong?

MONTANUS No, I do not, but I consider it a shame and a disgrace for me, a *Baccalaureus Philosophiae*, to repudiate what I once have publicly maintained and to commit an impropriety against the order to which I belong. My duty is to make sure that *ne quid detrimenti patiatur respublica philosophica*.[3]

PER But if you can be convinced that what you believe is wrong, do you even then consider it a sin to give up your opinion?

MONTANUS Prove to me that it is wrong, and do it *methodice*.

PER That's easy enough. Now, there are many upstanding people living in this town; first, your father-in-law, who single-handedly worked his way up by virtue of his pen; then, there's my humble self, who has been deacon here for fourteen years, and, then, our good man the bailiff here, besides the parish constable and many other respectable residents who have paid their taxes and land-rent in good times as well as bad.

MONTANUS This is going to be quite a *syllogismus*! So where's all this prattle getting you?

PER Now I'm coming to what I wanted to say. Just you go and ask all these fine residents of our town and see if any of them agrees with you that the earth is round. I know of course that one must believe what many say, rather than what one man alone says. *Ergo*, you are wrong.

---

[1] "Academic laws and laudable rules."
[2] Latin for "Sir." The right form here would be *Domine*.
[3] (Make sure that) "nothing detrimental happens to the republic of philosophy."

MONTANUS You can bring everyone around over here and let them oppose me in one matter after another, and I shall quiet them all. People like that can't have any opinions of their own—they can only believe what I and other people tell them.

PER But if you were to tell them that the moon was made of green cheese, should they believe that, too?

MONTANUS Of course, what else? Tell me, what is it people around here think you are?

PER They think that I'm a good, honest man and deacon here in town, which is true.

MONTANUS And I say it's a lie. I say that you are a rooster, and I shall prove it as clearly as two and three makes five.

PER The hell you will! What now, am I a rooster? How are you going to manage that?

MONTANUS Can you tell me something that proves you are not a rooster?

PER Well, first of all I can talk, and a rooster cannot talk; *ergo*, I am not a rooster.

MONTANUS Speech doesn't change matters. A parrot and starling can talk, but that doesn't make them human.

PER I can prove it with other things besides speech. A rooster has no reasoning ability; I have the ability to reason; *ergo*, I am not a rooster.

MONTANUS *Proba minorem.*[1]

JESPER No, speak Danish!

MONTANUS I want him to prove that he possesses the ability to reason.

PER Now, listen here, I manage the duties of my office beyond reproach, don't I?

MONTANUS What are the most difficult duties of your office by which you would prove that you possess the ability to reason?

PER First of all, I never forget to ring for service at the appointed hours.

---

1 "Prove the minor (proposition)."

MONTANUS Nor does a rooster forget to crow and let people know what time it is and when to get up.

PER Besides, I can sing as well as any deacon in the whole of Sjælland.

MONTANUS Our rooster, too, crows as well as any rooster in the whole of Sjaelland.

PER I can make wax candles; there's no rooster that can do that.

MONTANUS But a rooster on the other hand can make eggs, which you can't do. So you see, don't you, that the reasoning ability required in your office does not prove you to be any better than a rooster? And notice, too, in a nutshell, the similarities between yourself and a rooster. A rooster crows, you crow too; a rooster is proud of its voice and ruffles its feathers, you do the same; a rooster warns that it's time to get up, you give warning that it's time to go to mass. *Ergo*—you are a rooster. Do you have anything more to say for yourself? [Per weeps.]

JESPER Don't cry, Per. Surely you don't believe such nonsense?

PER I'll be damned if it isn't a downright lie. I can get papers from all over town proving that I'm not a rooster and that none of my ancestors have been anything but good Christians.

MONTANUS Then refute this *syllogismum, quem tibi propono*.[1] A rooster has the following qualities, by which it is distinguished from other animals; it warns people with its voice that they are to get up, it announces the hours and struts about because of its voice. You have the same qualities. *Ergo*—you are a rooster. [Per weeps again.]

JESPER If the deacon can't shut your mouth, then I can.

MONTANUS Let's hear your arguments then.

JESPER First of all, my conscience tells me that your opinion is wrong.

MONTANUS One can't always pass judgment according to the conscience of a bailiff.

JESPER Second, I say that all the things you've said here have been outright lies.

MONTANUS Prove it.

---

1 "This syllogism, which I present to you."

JESPER Third, I'm an upstanding man whose word has always been as good as truth.

MONTANUS With all this talk you'll convince no one.

JESPER In the fourth place, I say you have spoken like a heathen and that the tongue should be cut out of your mouth.

MONTANUS I still haven't heard any proof.

JESPER And fifth and last of all I'll give you more proof than you need by sword or bare knuckles.

MONTANUS I have respect for both, but so long as you wish to dispute with the mouth alone, you'll find that I can defend not only the things I've said but other things as well. Just come on, Mr. Bailiff, and I shall prove by sound *logica* that you are an ox.

JESPER The hell you will!

MONTANUS If you will only have the patience to hear my argument.

JESPER Come on, Per, let's go.

MONTANUS This is how I prove it. *Quicunque*…[1] [Jesper bellows and covers Montanus's mouth.] If you don't care to hear my proof now, you can meet me some other time, at whatever place you choose.

JESPER I'm too good to be associating with such a fanatic. [He leaves with the deacon.]

MONTANUS [Alone.] With these people I can dispute dispassionately however much they insult me. I don't get angry unless I'm disputing with people who imagine that they understand *methodum disputandi*[2] and are just as strong in philosophy as I. That's why I was ten times as agitated when I was disputing with that student today, who at least had some semblance of learning. But there come my parents.

---

1 "Whosoever…"
2 "Method of disputing."

Scene 3

(Jeppe, Nille, Montanus)

JEPPE Oh, my dear son, you mustn't get so worked up, and don't start quarreling with everybody. I hear that the bailiff and deacon, who at our request took it upon themselves to make peace between you and your father-in-law, have been made fun of. What's the good of that, turning people into oxen and roosters?

MONTANUS For this purpose I have studied, and for this purpose I have racked my brains: so that I may say whatever I choose, and defend it.

JEPPE Then it seems to me it would have been better never to have studied.

MONTANUS Shut your mouth, old man!

JEPPE Surely you wouldn't strike your parents?

MONTANUS If I did, I should defend it before the whole world. [Parents leave, weeping.]

Scene 4

(Montanus, Jacob)

MONTANUS I will not give up my opinions, even if it drives them all crazy. But what do you want, Jacob?

JACOB I have a letter for the Monsur. [Montanus takes the letter. Jacob leaves.]

MONTANUS [Alone, reads.] My dearest friend. I'd never have imagined that you so readily would forsake her who for so many years has borne you such a genuine and unerring love. I can tell you for certain that my father is so set against your idea that the earth is round and considers it so great an article of faith that he will never give me to you unless you accept the beliefs held by him and the other good people here in town. What difference can it make to you whether the earth is oblong, round, eight-sided, or rectangular? I beg you with all my love to conform to that faith which for such a long time has served us so well around here. If you do not comply with my wishes in this, know that I will die of grief, and that the entire world will despise you for having caused the death of one who has loved you as her own soul. —Elisabeth, daughter of Jeronimus. By her own hand. Oh heavens! This letter moves me and brings me in doubt, so that I must say with the poet

> *Utque securi*
> *Saucia, trabs ingens, ubi plaga novissima restat,*
> *Quo cadat, in dubio est, omnique a parte timetur,*
> *Sic animus…*[1]

On the one side stands philosophy, and demands that I stand firm; on the other, my sweetheart, who reproves me for being cold and unfaithful. But should Erasmus Montanus let anything move him to abandon his conviction, which hitherto has been his greatest virtue? Certainly not, never! Yet here is necessity, which knows no law. If I do not submit in this, I will make both myself and my sweetheart unhappy; she will fret and die of sorrow, and all the world will hate and upbraid me for having been unfaithful. Should I forsake her who for so many years has loved me so sincerely? Should I be the cause of her death? No, that must not come to pass. But consider what you do, *Erasme Montane, musarum et Apollinis pulle*.[2] Here you have the opportunity to prove that you are a true *philosophus*. The greater the danger, the greater laurel wreath do you win *inter philosophos*. Think what your *commilitones* will say when they hear, "He is no longer the Erasmus Montanus who defended his beliefs to the last drop of his blood." If vulgar and ignorant people reproach me for being unfaithful to my sweetheart, *philosophi* on the other hand will exalt me to the heavens. The very thing that brings me shame in the eyes of some causes others to crown me with honor. And so, I must resist this temptation. I resist it. I conquer it. I have already conquered it. The world is round. *Jacta est alea. Dixi.*[3] [Calls for Jacob.] Jacob! The letter you delivered from my sweetheart has had no effect on me. I stand by what I have said. The earth is round, and it shall never be flat as long as my head remains on my shoulder.

JACOB I, too, believe the earth is round, but if someone gave me a seedcake to say it was oblong, I would say it was oblong, because it's all the same to me.

MONTANUS That may be permissible for you, but not for a *philosopho*, whose principal virtue is to defend to the end what he once has said. I will

---

1 "Just as—when wounded by the axe and the last stroke remains—the powerful tree does not know to what side it will fall, so my conscience…" Quote from Ovid's *Metamorphosis*, Book 10, lines 372–75.
2 "Erasmus Montanus, favorite of the muses and of Apollo."
3 "The die has been cast. I have spoken."

publicly dispute on the subject here in town and challenge all who have studied.

JACOB But permit me to ask the Monsur about one thing. If you win the dispute, what then?

MONTANUS Then I will have the honor of winning and being regarded as a learned man.

JACOB Monsur means to say a talkative man, for I can tell by the people here in town that being talkative and being wise aren't the same thing. Rasmus Hansen, who is always talking and whose mouth can be stopped by no one, is thought to have only average goose intelligence. The parish constable Niels Christensen on the other hand, who says little and always yields his opinion, is considered competent to manage the office of chief bailiff.

MONTANUS Now listen to the rogue; I do believe he's trying his hand at reasoning!

JACOB Monsur mustn't be offended. I talk only from my limited understanding, and I ask only so that I can learn. I'd like to know if, when Monsur wins the dispute, Per the Deacon will then suddenly be changed into a rooster.

MONTANUS What nonsense! He'll remain exactly as he was.

JACOB Why, but then Monsur loses.

MONTANUS I've no intention of engaging in disputation with a peasant rogue. If you understood Latin, I'd satisfy you immediately—but I'm not accustomed to disputing in Danish.

JACOB Which is to say that the Monsur has become so learned he can no longer make himself understood in his mother tongue.

MONTANUS Shut your mouth, *audacissime juvenis*.[1] Why should I take the trouble of explaining myself to coarse and vulgar people who don't even know what *universalia, entia rationis* and *formae substantiales*[2] are, to say nothing of other things. Why it's *absurdissimum* to hold forth to the blind about colors. *Vulgus indoctum est monstrum horrendum informe, cui lumen adeptum.*[3] There was a man just the other day, easily ten times as learned

---

[1] "You audacious young man."
[2] "Universal concepts, imagined entities, and the eternal form of things."
[3] "The ignorant masses are a horrible formless monster, from whom light is withheld." Quote from Virgil's *Aeneid*, Book 3, line 658.

as you, who wanted to dispute with me, but because I noticed that he didn't know what *quidditas*[1] was, I promptly turned him down.

JACOB What does that mean anyway—*quidditas*, wasn't that it?

MONTANUS You can be sure I know what it means.

JACOB Perhaps Monsur does understand it himself but can't explain it to others. But what little I know, everyone can understand when I explain it to them.

MONTANUS Yes, you're a learned man, Jacob! What do you know?

JACOB And what if I could prove that I was more learned than the Monsur?

MONTANUS That I'd like to hear.

JACOB He who studies the most important things has, in my opinion, the greatest learning.

MONTANUS So you consider coarse peasant labor to be the most important?

JACOB I don't know about that, but this I do know, that if peasants, too, were to take a pen or piece of chalk in their hands and measure how far it is to the moon, you university men would soon hear your bellies complaining. You learned ones pass the time despeeting about whether the earth is round, square, or eight-sided, and we study how to keep the earth in order. Does Monsur now see that our studies are more useful and important than yours and that Niels Christensen is the most learned man here in town, because he has improved his land so that an acre's yield is worth five riksdalers more than in the day of his predecessor, who sat all day with a pipe in his mouth, besmudging and rumpling the pages of Doctor Arent Huitfeldt's chronicle or book of sermons?[2]

MONTANUS Oh, this is killing me! It's the devil incarnate speaking. I'd never in all my days suspected there were such words in the mouth of a peasant lad, because although everything you've said has been false and profane, still it was an uncommon speech for a man of your standing. Tell me this minute from whom you've learned such talk.

JACOB I haven't learned it, Monsur, but people say I've got a good head. The district judge never comes to town without sending for me at once.

---

1 Quiddity or "it-ness." See Introduction, p. vi.
2 Arild Huitfeldt (1546–1609), who was no doctor, wrote a history (chronicle) of Denmark, but no book of sermons.

A hundred times he has told my parents that they should hold me to my books and that I could amount to something. When I don't have anything to do, I go around thinking. Just the other day I composed a verse on Morten Nielsen, who drank himself to death.

MONTANUS Let me hear that verse.

JACOB First you have to know that this same Morten's father and grandfather were both fishermen and drowned at sea. The verse went like this: Under this stone Morten Nielsen rests. / To tread in his forebears' footsteps, / Who as fishermen died at sea, / He drowned himself in brandy. / I had to read the verse the other day for the district judge, who had it written down and gave me two marks for it.

MONTANUS The verse, although it is *formaliter* very poor, is nonetheless *materialiter* quite excellent. The prosody, which is most important, is lacking.

JACOB What does that mean?

MONTANUS Some of the lines do not have enough *pedes*, or feet, to walk on.

JACOB Feet! Why I'll have you know that in just a couple of days it's traveled all over the country.

MONTANUS I can see that you have a shrewd mind, I only wish you had studied and understood your *philosophiam instrumentalem* then you could have studied under me. Come on, let's go. [They leave.]

ACT V

Scene 1

(A Lieutenant, Jesper, The Bailiff)

LIEUTENANT Where can I get a look at this fellow, Mr. Bailiff? I'd like to have a word with him. Does he look all right?

JESPER Sure, he looks fine and has a tongue as sharp as a razor.

LIEUTENANT That makes no difference so long as he's strong and healthy.

JESPER He can say whatever he chooses and defend it. He proved beyond a doubt that Per the Deacon was a rooster.

LIEUTENANT Is he fairly broad across the shoulders?

JESPER A strong able-bodied fellow. Everyone in the household is afraid of him, even his parents, because he can turn them into cows, oxen, and horses and then back into people again—that is, he proves according to the books that that's what they are.

LIEUTENANT Does he look like he can endure hardship?

JESPER He also proved that the earth is round.

LIEUTENANT That's none of my concern, but does he appear to be brave and stouthearted?

JESPER He'd put his life on the line for a letter of the alphabet, to say nothing of other things. I'm sure he'll have all the people around here on his neck, but that doesn't bother him, and he won't give up his opinions and learning because of it.

LIEUTENANT Mr. Bailiff, from what I hear, he should make the perfect soldier.

JESPER How are you going to turn him into a soldier? He's a student.[1]

---
1 Students were exempted from military service.

LIEUTENANT That makes no difference. If he can turn people into sheep, oxen, and roosters, then for once I'll try to turn a student into a soldier.

JESPER I wish you would; I'd laugh till my sides split.

LIEUTENANT Just keep quiet about it, Jesper. When the bailiff and lieutenant put their heads together, these things aren't impossible. But there I see someone coming. Could that be him?

JESPER Yes, that's him. I'll be off, so that he doesn't suspect me.

Scene 2

(Lieutenant, Montanus)

LIEUTENANT With all due respect, I congratulate you upon your arrival here in town.

MONTANUS I humbly thank you.

LIEUTENANT I've taken the liberty of seeking out your company, since there are so few educated people around here a man can talk to.

MONTANUS I'm pleased to hear you have studied. And when, Sir, did you graduate, if I may inquire?

LIEUTENANT I graduated ten years ago.

MONTANUS Why, then, you are an old *academicus*. And what was your field of study when you were a student?

LIEUTENANT I read mostly the old Latin authors and studied natural law[1] and moral questions, which I still do.

MONTANUS Ah, but that's just tinsel, not *academicum*. Didn't you place any emphasis on *philosophiam instrumentalem*?

LIEUTENANT No, none in particular.

MONTANUS So you've never disputed?

LIEUTENANT No.

---
[1] Holberg was particularly interested in natural law and published a book on the subject in 1716.

MONTANUS No? And that's studying? *Philosophia instrumentalis* is the only substantial field of study; the rest can be fine enough, but not learned. One who is well-versed in *logica* and *metaphysica* can get himself out of any difficulty and dispute on all matters, even if they are unfamiliar to him. I don't know a single subject for which I could not argue the defense and come out on top. There was never a disputation at the university in which I did not participate as opponent. A *philosophus* can pass for a *polyhistor*.[1]

LIEUTENANT Who is the best disputant these days?

MONTANUS A student named Per Iversen. When he has refuted his opponent so thoroughly that he hasn't a word left to say for himself, he says: "Will you now take my position, and I in turn shall defend yours." For that sort of thing his *philosophia instrumentalis* is particularly helpful. It's a shame the fellow didn't become a lawyer; he would have had quite an income. After him, I am the best, for last time I disputed he whispered in my ear: "*Jam sumus ergo pares.*"[2] Nonetheless, I shall always defer to him.

LIEUTENANT But I've heard it said that Monsieur can prove that it is the duty of children to beat their parents.

MONTANUS If I said that, I'm man enough to defend it.

LIEUTENANT I dare wager a ducat that you can't.

MONTANUS I'll wager a ducat against you.

LIEUTENANT Fine, then that's agreed, now let's hear.

MONTANUS He whom one loves the most, one beats the most.[3] A man should love no one more than his parents—*ergo*, he should beat them the most. Or, according to another *syllogismo*, what I have been given I should, to the best of my ability, give in return. I have during my childhood received blows from my parents, *ergo*, I should give them blows in return.

LIEUTENANT Enough, enough, I've lost! You shall certainly have your ducat.

MONTANUS No, you weren't being serious—I *profecto* won't take the money.

LIEUTENANT Indeed, Sir, you shall; I swore upon it.

---

1 A person learned in many fields.
2 "So we are already equals."
3 Cf. the Bible (several places): "Whom the Lord loveth, him he chasteneth."

MONTANUS Then I will take the money, but only so that you may avoid breaking your oath.

LIEUTENANT But mightn't I also see if I can't turn you into something? For example, I will turn you into a soldier.

MONTANUS Oh that's easy. All students are intellectual soldiers.

LIEUTENANT No, I shall prove that you are bodily a soldier. Whoever has accepted conscription money is an enlisted soldier. You have done so…

MONTANUS *Nego minorem.*[1]

LIEUTENANT *Et ego probo minorem*[2] by the two riksdalers I put in your hand.

MONTANUS *Distinguendum est inter nummos.*[3]

LIEUTENANT There's no distinction. You are a soldier.

MONTANUS *Distinguendum est inter to simpliciter et relative accipere.*[4]

LIEUTENANT Nonsense! The contract is closed, and you have received your money.

MONTANUS *Distinguemnum est inter contractum verum et apparentem.*[5]

LIEUTENANT Can you deny that you received two riksdalers from me?

MONTANUS *Distinguendum est inter rem et modum rei.*[6]

LIEUTENANT Come on, follow me on the double, comrade. Now you are going to get your uniform.

MONTANUS There's your two riksdalers back again. And, besides, you have no witness to my taking the money.

---

[1] "I deny the minor (proposition)."
[2] "I prove the minor (proposition)."
[3] "It is necessary to distinguish between [kinds of] money."
[4] "It is necessary to distinguish between accepting money generally and, on the other hand, for some special purpose."
[5] "It is necessary to distinguish between a true and a simulated contract."
[6] "It is necessary to distinguish between the thing itself and its outer appearance."

Scene 3

(Jesper, Niels, The Corporal, Montanus, The Lieutenant)

JESPER I can testify to seeing the lieutenant put the money into his hand.

NIELS I, too.

MONTANUS But why did I take the money? *Distinguendum est inter…*

LIEUTENANT Come now, we don't want to hear any more of this talk. Niels, you stay here while I get the uniform. [He leaves.]

MONTANUS Oh, help!

NIELS Shut up, you dog, or I'll stab you in the belly with my bayonet. He's enlisted, isn't he, Mr. Bailiff?

JESPER Yes, that's true enough.

LIEUTENANT [Returning.] Come on, hurry up, take that black coat off and put on this red one. [Montanus weeps as they put on his uniform.] Oh, come now, it does not look good for a soldier to be crying—you're much better off now than you were before. Now drill him well, Niels. He's a learned fellow, but he's still a tenderfoot when it comes to exercises. [Niels the Corporal leads Montanus off, drilling and beating him. The Lieutenant and Jesper leave.]

Scene 4

(Lieutenant, Niels, Montanus)

LIEUTENANT Well, Niels, how does he manage the drills?

NIELS He'll learn. He's a lazy dog, though, and has to be beaten every minute.

MONTANUS [Weeping.] Oh, gracious Sir, have mercy on me. I have a frail constitution and cannot endure such treatment.

LIEUTENANT It seems a bit rough at first, but when your back has been sufficiently beaten and toughened, it won't hurt so much.

MONTANUS Oh, would that I had never studied, then I'd never have gotten into this predicament.

LIEUTENANT Oh, but this is only the beginning. When you've sat half a score times on the wooden horse or stood on the stake once, you'll think this sort of thing is just a trifle. [Montanus weeps again.]

Scene 5

(Jeronimus, Magdelone, Lisbet, Jeppe, Nille, Lieutenant, Montanus, Niels)

JERONIMUS Are you quite sure about that?

JEPPE Yes, quite. The bailiff told me just now. Oh, now my anger is changed to sympathy.

JERONIMUS If we could make a true believer of him again, I'd gladly buy him free.

LISBET [Rushing in.] Oh, what a miserable wretch I am!

JERONIMUS Don't make such a fuss, daughter; you won't gain anything by that.

LISBET Oh, my dear father, if you were as much in love as I am, you wouldn't tell me to keep quiet.

JERONTMUS Shame! It's not proper for a girl to show her feelings like that. But I do believe that's him standing over there. Listen, Rasmus Berg, what's going on?

MONTANUS Oh, my dear Monsieur Jeronimus, I've become a soldier.

JERONIMUS Well, now you'll have other things to busy yourself with besides changing people into animals and deacons into roosters.

MONTANUS Ah, I lament my former folly, but all too late.

JERONIMUS Listen, my friend. If you will give up your former foolishness and not go starting quarrels and disputations all over the place, I shall not fail to do everything in my power to get you free again.

MONTANUS Oh, I don't deserve better, I who have threatened to beat my parents. But if you will take pity on me and try to get me free, I swear to you that I will henceforth lead a different life, take up some business, and never again trouble anyone with disputations.

JERONIMUS Then stay here for a moment; I shall go and speak with the Lieutenant. Ah, my dear Lieutenant. You have always been a friend of our household; the person you have enlisted as a soldier is engaged to my only daughter, who loves him deeply. Set him free again, and I shall gladly present you with a hundred riksdalers. I confess that I was pleased at first to see him punished in this manner, since his peculiar behavior has gotten me and all the good people here in town up in arms against him. But when I saw him in this plight and at the same time heard him lament his former folly and promise to mend his ways, my heart nearly burst with sympathy.

LIEUTENANT Listen, my dear Monsieur Jeronimus. What I have done is only for his own good. I know that he is engaged to your daughter and have therefore, for the purpose alone of serving your household, reduced him to this condition and treated him with such severity that he might repent his sins. But I will, for your sake, give the money to the poor, since I'm told that he really has had a change of heart. Just let him come here... Listen, my friend. Your parents have spent a lot of money on you, in hopes that you would be an honor and a comfort to them in their old age; but you go off a sensible lad and come back entirely deranged, provoke the whole village, and advocate strange ideas, which you stubbornly defend. If that's to be the fruit of studying, one should wish that there had never been any books at all. It seems to me that the most important thing one ought to learn in the schools is precisely the opposite of what you've been doing, and that a learned man should above all distinguish himself from others in being more temperate, modest, and open-minded in his utterances than the uneducated. For true philosophy teaches us that we should restrain and silence quarrels and concede our opinions as soon as we're convinced—even by the humblest of men—that we are mistaken. The first law of philosophy is "Know thyself," and the further one has progressed, the lower opinion one has of one's self and the more, it will then seem, there remains to be learned. But you turn philosophy into a game of fencing and maintain that a philosopher is a person who by subtle distinctions can distort the truth and argue his way out of any opinion. By so doing, you incur the hatred of people and bring contempt upon learning, since people imagine your extraordinary behavior to be the true fruit of education. The best advice I can give you is that you strive to forget and to clear your head of all that which you sat up so many nights to learn, and that you take up some business in which you can work your way up or, if you insist upon pursuing your studies, that you go about them in some other fashion.

MONTANUS Oh, gracious Sir, I shall follow your advice and endeavor to become a different person hereafter.

LIEUTENANT Good! Then I will let you go as soon as you have given that promise to your own parents, as well as to your parents-in-law, and begged their forgiveness.

MONTANUS I beg you all humbly and in tearful supplication to forgive me, and I promise to lead an entirely different life hereafter. I condemn my former ways, from which I am rescued, not only by the circumstances I have fallen into but also by this man's thorough advice and profound wisdom, and for this, I shall always hold him, next after my parents, in the highest esteem.

JERONIMUS So, do you no longer maintain, my dear son-in-law, that the earth is round? For that is the point that weighs most heavily on my heart.

MONTANUS My dear father-in-law, I will dispute no further on that matter. This alone I will say: that all learned people these days are of the opinion that the earth is round.

JERONIMUS Oh ... Mr. Lieutenant, let him become a soldier again until the earth becomes flat.

MONTANUS My dear father-in-law, the earth is as flat as a pancake. Are you now satisfied?

JERONIMUS Yes, now we're good friends again, and you shall have my daughter. Now all of you must come to my house and drink a toast of reconciliation. Mr. Lieutenant, do us the honor of joining us. [They all go inside.]

END